At 5:04 on the morning of April 18, 1906, the people of San Francisco were awakened by an earthquake. Gas lamps tipped, stoves toppled, electric wires broke, gas mains cracked, and water lines burst. Many buildings in the city of San Francisco were destroyed by the fires that erupted because of the earthquake.

Following the earthquake, a tent city was set up in Golden Gate Park for people who had lost their homes, and in the days that followed citizens banded together to clean up and rebuild their city. During this time, a small terrier was found in the basement of the fire-damaged St. Francis Hotel. The dog became a celebrity, his picture even appeared in the newspaper, and he was named Francis. It is also true that Enrico Caruso was visiting San Francisco at the time of the Earthquake. The rest of this story is just that: a *story*.

For Panda and Dalai and in memory of Patches and Duffy –JE & ST

Dedicated to Andy Lorea Reda and Wissim Bouayadi –BS

Special thanks to Victoria Rock, Suellen Ehnebuske, Laura Lovett and the wonderful staff at Chronicle Books. –BS

Text © 1996 Judith Ross Enderle and Stephanie Gordon Tessler.
Illustrations © 1996 Brooke Scudder.
All rights reserved.

Book design by Suellen Ehnebuske and Joyce Marie Kuchar
Typeset in Palatino BQ, and Heatwave

Printed in Hong Kong.

10 9 8 7 6 5 4 3 2

Chronicle Books LLC
85 Second Street
San Francisco, CA 94105

www.chroniclekids.com

Library of Congress Cataloging-in-Publication Data:
Enderle, Judith A.
    Francis, the earthquake dog / by Judith Ross Enderle and
    Tessler, Stephanie G.; illustrated by Brooke Scudder.
        p.   cm.
Summary: In 1906, in the aftermath of the San Francisco earthquake,
Edward searches for the mischievous stray dog with which he has fallen in
love.
1. Earthquakes—California—San Francisco—Juvenile fiction.
[1. Earthquakes—California—San Francisco—Fiction.
2. Dogs—Fiction.   3. San Francisco (Calif.)—Fiction.]
I. Tessler, Stephanie Gordon.   II. Scudder, Brooke, ill.
III. Title. PZ7.E6965Fr 1996
     [E]—dc20   94-46644

        CIP   AC

FRANCIS
The Earthquake Dog

by Judith Ross Enderle & Stephanie Gordon Tessler

Illustrated by Brooke Scudder

CHRONICLE BOOKS · SAN FRANCISCO

Edward raced up the steep San Francisco hill. Papa would be upset if he was late again.

Automobiles honked. Cable cars clanged. Carriage wheels clattered.

Suddenly, a little dog ran in front of a vegetable cart. The cart horse reared. Tomatoes, potatoes, and cabbages tumbled downhill.

As the cart driver shouted, Edward scooped up the quivering dog. "Don't worry," he whispered. "I'll take care of you."

At the St. Francis Hotel, Papa was waiting. His mustache drooped a little. His chef's hat shook. "You are late!" he roared. "And no dogs allowed in my kitchen."

"Please, Papa," Edward begged. "He's lost."

The little dog wagged his tail until Papa's mustache curled upward.

"**P**ut him in the cellar. Hurry! You must set the tables. Tonight is the grand party for Enrico Caruso, the famous opera singer."

"Yes, Papa. Thank you, Papa." Edward shut the cellar door.

Woo, woo, woo, cried the little dog.

"Do I hear Enrico Caruso, the great opera singer?" the pastry cook teased.

"Get to work," said Papa, "or we will be singing sad songs when the food isn't ready."

Edward washed his hands. Just as he was picking up a stack of china plates, the sauce chef opened the cellar door and the little dog raced out. "Stop!" shouted Edward.

"Get that dog!" shouted Papa.

Edward ran after the little dog, but there was no little dog in the pantry. There was no little dog in the dumbwaiter.

There was no little dog in the laundry room.

Suddenly a scream came from the lobby of the hotel.

Edward ran faster.

"**W**ho let this dog in here?" demanded the manager. His stiff collar stood at attention. "No dogs allowed in my hotel."

Edward ducked behind a potted palm. His heart was racing. The little dog was in big trouble now.

Woof! Woof! Woof! barked the little dog.

A lady wearing a feathered hat hid behind the bell hop.

The bell hop hid behind the manager.

"Shoo! Shoo! Shoo!" the manager cried.

Edward reached for the little dog. The palm tipped over.

"Look what you've done," shouted the hotel manager. His face turned as red as raspberries. The lady with the feathered hat scurried to the elevator. Then a man, as round as a barrel, strode through the lobby and stepped in after her. The little dog dashed into the elevator, too.

The man's voice rang out like a church bell. "UP, PLEASE!"

"Wait!" shouted Edward, but the elevator door slid shut.

Edward raced up the hotel stairs. The little dog wasn't on the first floor.

He wasn't on the second floor. He wasn't on any of the floors in the St. Francis Hotel.

Edward scuffed back to the kitchen. The sauce chef's savory broth bubbled. The sweet smell of the pastry chef's lemon tarts tickled Edward's nose. But there was no little dog in the kitchen, either.

"You've broken six plates," Papa said with a sniffle as he diced onions. "And you've lost a dog in the St. Francis Hotel." His mustache drooped way down.

"I'm sorry," Edward said. He wiped away an onion tear. "I've looked everywhere."

"Later, you will look some more," said Papa. "Now you must set the tables."

In the dining room, Edward placed three forks, three spoons and three knives by each plate. While he worked, Edward worried about the little dog.

That evening, while Papa directed the hustle and bustle in the kitchen, Edward snuck into the lobby. Excited whispers swept through the crowd when Mr. Enrico Caruso made his grand entrance. The opera singer was the same man who had gotten on the elevator that afternoon! Maybe he knew where the little dog was. Edward inched forward.

"Mr. Caruso, please sing for us," begged a lady.

"Please, sir…," Edward began, hoping the great Mr. Enrico Caruso would tell him where the little dog had gone.

Mr. Caruso looked down. "For the boy then, a few *fantastico* notes." The singer spread his arms. His voice echoed like thunder. The last note was so long, Edward felt out of breath. Then the great opera singer was swallowed up by the crowd before Edward had a chance to ask about the little dog.

Very late that night, Edward and Papa climbed the stairs of their boarding house. Papa's mustache curled way up. Mr. Caruso's grand party had made Papa forget about the little dog and Edward didn't remind him.

With nightshirts on, they climbed into the squeaky brass bed. Edward prayed, "Hello to Mama, who is with the angels. Please bless Papa. Help me be smart in school. And," he whispered, "please let me find the little dog. Amen." The sputter and stomp of horses and the howling of dogs carried on the night air. Beside him, Papa snored. Edward finally fell asleep, worrying about the little dog.

Suddenly the big brass bed bounced and Papa and Edward tumbled out. The boarding house rocked like a boat in the ocean.

"Don't be afraid," said Papa, hugging Edward. "I have you."

"And I have you," said Edward, hugging Papa.

The ground rumbled and their bed slid across the floor.

When the shaking stopped, Papa grabbed Edward's hand and his chef's hat, and they ran outside. Papa looked funny wearing his nightgown and chef's hat, but Edward didn't laugh.

"Earthquake! Earthquake!" someone shouted. People rushed about. Glass, wood, and bricks were strewn everywhere. Water lines burst. Electric lines snapped. The smoky morning sky was awash in red as fires spread through San Francisco.

It took Edward and Papa a long time to make their way safely to Golden Gate Park. Houses and buildings lay in crumbled heaps. Edward worried more than ever about the little dog.

Days passed. Papa and Edward lived in an army tent. Edward carried buckets of water and Papa made earthquake stew and bonfire biscuits for hungry people who stood in long lines. Once Edward heard barking. "Here, little dog," he called. But it wasn't his little dog.

Papa's mustache drooped all the time, now. "I don't have a kitchen," he said. "We don't have a boarding house. We don't even have a city."

"But we have each other," said Edward.

Papa's mustache lifted just a little. He hugged Edward. "You are right. We have each other. That is most important."

Soon many people were working to rebuild San Francisco. Edward and Papa carried books from the tumbled down library to a warehouse, where the books would be stored, until the new library could be built. They cleared away bricks that covered the cable car tracks. And they helped haul rubble from the St. Francis Hotel. The hotel had survived the earthquake but had been damaged in the fire.

Edward found the brass bell from the desk in the lobby. He found three keys and one silver fork. Suddenly, Edward heard… *woo, woo, woo*. "Papa!" he shouted. "We must dig!"

They pushed. They pulled. They tugged. And they dug.

"I see him!" Edward shouted when a tiny black nose poked from ur a heap. Hands heaved rubble into high piles until at last the little do scrambled from the basement of the St. Francis Hotel.

Edward scooped him up and the little dog licked his face. "May I keep him, Papa. Please?" he asked.

Papa patted the little dog. "You'll take care of him?"

"Oh yes, Papa," said Edward.

"You won't lose him?"

"Oh no, Papa," said Edward. "And I'll call him Francis, after your hotel—Francis the Earthquake Dog." Papa's mustache curved way up.

Woof! Woof! Woof! barked Francis the Earthquake Dog.

All about Earthquakes

The surface of the earth is made up of rocky plates. There are seven large plates and several smaller ones. These plates move slowly back and forth against each other. The rocks along the edges of the plates get squeezed burying old ground and causing new mountains to begin to form and stretch. If the plates press too hard against each other, or break or shift suddenly, there is an earthquake.

The energy released when the plates shift or break is called seismic energy. This energy travels in waves causing the earth to shake or quake. Some waves make the ground jump up and down and others make the ground slide back and forth.

Earthquakes happen all the time, but most are deep under the sea or far below the earth's surface and people can't feel them. Earthquakes occur in many parts of the world. In the United States earthquakes have been recorded in all fifty states since 1755. While some places are more likely to experience earthquakes, it is a good idea for everyone to know what to do when an earthquake strikes.

What To Do When There's An Earthquake:

1. Most important: Stay Calm. Take action at the first sign of an earthquake.

2. If there's an adult with you, follow instructions.

3. At school, get under a desk or table. Stay away from windows. On the school bus, stay seated and hold on.

4. At home, get under a heavy table or sit in an inside doorway. Stay away from windows.

5. Outside, try to find a clear open space away from buildings, electric poles, and trees. Be especially careful not to touch any fallen wires. Lie down or crouch near the ground.

6. When the shaking is over, if you are alone, try to find an adult. Be sure you are wearing shoes and if the lights go out, use a flashlight but never a candle.

7. Avoid leaking water, broken wires, and broken glass.

8. To find out more about earthquakes and what to do during an earthquake, talk to your parents, your teachers, and look in your library for more books about earthquakes.

Earth is our one and only planet
to care for, love, and preserve.

Today our Earth faces big challenges. Human activity has been causing the climate to change and become warmer. Climate change affects people, plants, and animals everywhere. Below are a few Internet resources to help you learn more about climate and how you can take care of our one and only Earth. Maybe you can begin by planting a tree!

Arbor Day Foundation
arborday.org

Center for Climate and Energy Solutions: Climate Basics for Kids
c2es.org/content/climate-basics-for-kids

Earth Day
earthday.org

Fridays for Future: *Learn about the movement begun by climate activist Greta Thunberg when she was fifteen.*
fridaysforfuture.org

NASA Climate Kids
climatekids.nasa.gov/climate-change-meaning

NASA Kids' Club
nasa.gov/kidsclub/index.html

National Geographic Kids
kids.nationalgeographic.com

One. Only one.
The story ends where it began,
with only one.

One. Only one.
Earth is our one and only planet
to care for, love, and preserve.

Yet together we are part
of one human family
and the great diversity of life.

TREE
PLANTING DAY

But though there are seven billion of us,
we are each unique,
with bodies, brains, fingerprints,
and feelings all our own.
Around the world,
people wear different clothes,
eat different foods,
and speak many languages.

TREE
PLANTI

Our Earth holds all this life,
along with us—
more than seven billion human beings.

Some are too small to see with our eyes,
so we use a microscope.

and nine hundred thousand species of bugs.
It has trees great and small,
flowers of all colors,
vegetables, mosses, mushrooms, mammals,
and thousands of tiny, tiny creatures.

Eight million seven hundred thousand
different kinds of creatures live on Earth.
We call each kind of creature a *species*.

Earth has more than
ten thousand species of birds,
twenty-five thousand species of fish . . .

canyons,

and rain forests.

It has mountains, deserts, 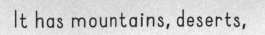 islands, volcanoes,

five great bodies of water called *oceans*;
and many rivers, lakes, and streams.

Earth also has seven huge pieces
of land called *continents*;

The Earth has a special layer around it
that makes it possible
for us to breathe,
for rain to fall,
and for plants to grow.
We call this layer the *atmosphere*.

Some have balls called *moons*
that orbit around them.
Earth has only one.
We call it, simply, *the moon*.

The eight planets and their moons
all orbit the sun.
So do a few small dwarf planets,
rocks called *asteroids*,
and comets—snowballs with long tails of
frozen gases, rock, and dust.
We call the sun and all these
swirling, zooming objects our *solar system*.

Jupiter

Saturn

Uranus

Neptune

We call the other planets
Mercury, Venus, Mars, Jupiter,
Saturn, Uranus, and Neptune.

Mercury   Venus   Earth   Mars

Eight large spinning balls
circle, or orbit, the sun.
We call these balls *planets*.
Only one is our home,
our one and only planet.
We call it *Earth*.

Only one star is close enough
to give us warmth and light.
We call this star our *sun*.

FOREST PARK

But during the day,
only one bright star shines in the sky.

The Milky Way contains at least
a hundred billion stars.
Most are so far away,
we can only see them through a telescope.
Even on the darkest night,
we're lucky if we can see
four thousand stars with our own eyes.

There may be
two trillion galaxies in the universe,
or even more.
Some have names that match their shapes:

Cartwheel

and Sunflower;

Sombrero

and Tadpole.

Only one galaxy is our home.
We call our home the *Milky Way.*

All through the vast sea of space,
gigantic clusters of stars
light up the darkness.
We call these star clusters *galaxies*.

Our universe contains
so many hot and glowing balls,
no one can count them all.
To us they look like
small bright points of light
twinkling in the sky.
We call these points of light *stars*.

BANG

to become EVERYTHING.
We call this everything
our *universe*.

A long, long time ago—
nearly fourteen billion years—
one tiny speck exploded with a . . .

One. Only one.
The story starts with one.

ONLY ONE

Written by **Deborah Hopkinson**   Illustrated by **Chuck Groenink**

a·s·b
anne schwartz books

For Greta Thunberg, who showed us all what only one can do,
and to young activists and tree planters everywhere
—D.H.

This book is for every kid who has started a conversation with "Did you know . . . ?"
—C.G.

Text copyright © 2022 by Deborah Hopkinson
Jacket art and interior illustrations copyright © 2022 by Chuck Groenink

All rights reserved. Published in the United States by Anne Schwartz Books,
an imprint of Random House Children's Books, a division of Penguin Random House LLC, New York.

Anne Schwartz Books and the colophon are trademarks of Penguin Random House LLC.

Visit us on the Web! rhcbooks.com

Educators and librarians, for a variety of teaching tools, visit us at RHTeachersLibrarians.com

Library of Congress Cataloging-in-Publication Data
Names: Hopkinson, Deborah, author. | Groenink, Chuck, illustrator.
Title: Only one / by Deborah Hopkinson; illustrated by Chuck Groenink.
Description: First edition. | New York: Anne Schwartz Books, an imprint of Random House Children's Books,
a division of Penguin Random House LLC, 2022. | Audience: Ages 4–8.
Summary: "This picture book showcases the unique beauty of our one-and-only universe—
its galaxies, stars, and planets—as well as our one-and-only Earth, and the precious life it contains"—Provided by publisher.
Identifiers: LCCN 2021008867 | ISBN 978-0-399-55703-3 (hardcover) | ISBN 978-0-399-55704-0 (lib. bdg.) | ISBN 978-0-399-55705-7 (ebook)
Subjects: LCSH: Cosmology—Juvenile literature. | Astronomy—Juvenile literature. | Picture books for children. |
Universe—Juvenile literature. | LCGFT: Picture books.
Classification: LCC QB983.H58 2022 | DDC 523.1—dc23

The text of this book is set in 18-point Cabrito Norm Medium and 17.5-point Catalina Clemente.
The illustrations were rendered in acrylic paint, ink, and Photoshop.
Book design by Nicole de las Heras

MANUFACTURED IN CHINA
10 9 8 7 6 5 4 3 2 1
First Edition